JUNGLES

ANGELA WILKES

Illustrated by
PETER DENNIS

Contents

Consultants: Operation Drake

In the Jungle

Jungles are thick, green forests which grow in hot, wet countries. They are also called rain forests because it rains nearly every day.

Near the equator, where jungles grow, there is no summer or winter. It is warm all year. Jungle trees are always green and grow very tall.

The trees and plants grow towards the light. They have flowers and fruit all year round.

There are many rivers in jungles because it rains so much.

2

Where there is sun, plants grow huge leaves. Some have hooks which catch on your clothes.

Many trees grow flowers and fruit on their trunks, like this South American cannonball tree.

Old giant trees die and crash to the ground. Young trees spring up in their places.

Termites look like white ants. They eat dead wood and build their nests on trees.

Leaf-cutting ants take bits of leaf back to their nest. They grow fungus on them to eat.

A lot of fungus grows in the jungle. It helps rot down dead plants to make new plant food.

Where the Animals Live

When you are walking in the jungle, you cannot see the higher treetops, nor the animals that live in them.

Here you can see what size the different trees are, and find out which animals live there.

The tallest trees look like giant umbrellas. They shelter the jungle from the sun, rain and wind.

This level is called the canopy. Most of the flowers and fruit grow here.

The short trees grow so close together that very little sunlight can get through them.

It is quite gloomy at ground level. Only small plants grow here.

Large birds, such as monkey-eating eagles, fly at this height, looking out for prey.

Most birds live at this level. So do animals that climb and jump, such as monkeys. They eat fruit and leaves.

The trees are very thick here and hard to move through. Small animals and birds live in them.

Large animals that cannot climb trees and many insects live on the jungle floor.

To find out more about life in the treetops, scientists build observation platforms.

They also build high walkways, so that they can look at birds and flowers more closely.

Moving through the Trees

These South American spider monkeys use their tails to help them grip on to branches.

When a baby monkey cannot jump between branches, its mother makes a bridge for it.

The monkeys leap from one tree to another, looking for leaves and fruit they can eat.

1

2

3

Gibbons live in the Asian jungles. They are apes. These look like monkeys without tails.

Gibbons are great acrobats. They have very long arms and strong, hooked fingers.

They swing from hand to hand through the branches of trees at a tremendous speed.

Some tree frogs look as if they can fly. Their webbed feet help them to glide when they jump.

The Asian flying lemur hangs upside down from the branch of a tree and sleeps during the day.

At night it looks for food. Flaps of skin between its limbs help it to glide like a kite.

'Flying' lizards also live in Asian jungles. When still, they look like ordinary lizards.

But when they jump, two flaps on their sides open out, and they can glide for a long way.

This Asian snake is called a flying snake. It can glide from one tree branch to another.

9

The Jungle at Night

Many jungle animals sleep all day and feed at night. As night falls, the jungle becomes very noisy. Howler monkeys start to call.

Frogs and toads gather in swamps and pools. They have very loud voices. They croak and squeak, hoping to attract a mate.

Many small animals go to drink at water holes at night. They all have different ways of protecting themselves from enemies.

The pangolin is an anteater with horny scales that are like armour. The moon rat smells bad, and the tiny mouse deer can run very fast.

Fruit-eating bats hang upside-down in trees. They sleep during the day and feed at night.

The world's biggest bats, they are also called flying foxes because of their faces.

Some flowers bloom only at night. They are white and strongly scented to attract moths.

Like many animals that come out at night, the loris has big eyes to help it see in the dark.

Male fireflies show off to female fireflies at night, by glowing with brilliant lights.

The River Amazon

The Amazon is one of the biggest rivers in the world. It is really many rivers joined together.

Lots of birds and animals live along the banks of the rivers, or go there to drink and find food.

A giant water lily grows in backwaters.

Hoatzin

Spoonbills wade in shallow water, looking for fish to catch.

The hoatzin is an odd bird. It can not fly very well but it can swim. The baby birds have claws on their wings to help them climb trees.

The caiman is a kind of alligator. It drifts along in the water, ready to snap at any fish and turtles it can eat.

Hummingbirds

Hummingbirds are tiny. One kind is no bigger than a bee. They live in the American jungles.

They beat their wings so fast that they make a humming noise. They hover when they feed.

Most hummingbirds have long beaks. They poke them into flowers to suck out the nectar.

Birds of paradise were given their name because of their beauty. The males are brilliantly coloured, but the females are plain and brown.

The males put on a show for the females, to help them choose their mates. They shriek, puff out their chests and show off their plumes.

Living in the Jungle – 1

Parts of the world's jungles are so hard to travel through that they have not been explored. But tribes have lived in the jungles for thousands of years, seeing no one from the outside world. Their way of life has not changed much since the Stone Age.

The pygmies live deep in the African jungles. They do not grow crops but collect wild plants to eat and hunt animals.

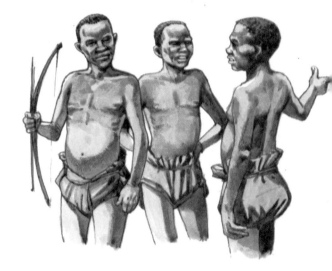

The pygmies are small and can move quickly and quietly through the forest. They pick up any food they find and tuck it into their belts.

Pygmies live in small family tribes. They move from place to place, staying in each one for as long as they can find food there.

They set up their camps in clearings. The women make huts out of young trees and big leaves. Each hut has a fire in front of it.

The men hunt with bows and poison-tipped arrows. They also catch animals in huge nets.

The women cook vegetable stews. They add any meat that has been killed.

Afterwards the men sit round a fire, telling stories and singing songs about the forest.

Living in the Jungle – 2

Some jungle tribes grow food as well as hunt. They cut down trees to make a clearing in the forest and then plant vegetables.

They build a village and fence in the crops to keep out animals. They stay in one village until no more crops will grow, then move on.

Some tribes in New Guinea keep wild pigs they have tamed, and treat them like pets.

In South America women grate, dry and sieve roots to make flour for a type of bread.

Tribes who live near the Amazon fish as well as hunt. These men are making a dug-out canoe.

Maloca

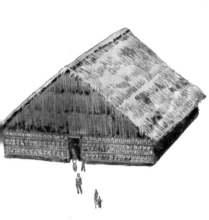

Some tribes build very unusual houses. A whole tribe lives in this South American maloca.

Stilt house

Some houses in South-East Asia are built on stilts, to help keep them dry and cool.

Haus tambaran

This is a special kind of religious house in Papua New Guinea. Only men are allowed in it.

Life is changing for jungle tribes. Many are now using money, and the children go to school.

Old tribal customs, such as war dances, are often only put on as shows for visiting tourists.

People now make money by growing crops to sell abroad, such as rubber and cocoa.

Jungle Killers

Hunters rely on speed, strength and camouflage to catch their food. The harpy eagle glides silently among the tree-tops, looking for animals.

When it sees a group of small monkeys, the eagle swoops down very fast. It seizes one of them in its claws, as it tries to escape.

Big cats creep up quietly on their victims and ambush them. Their spotted or striped coats are good camouflage in the jungle.

Although it can run fast, a jaguar cannot chase its prey a long way. So it creeps as close as it can, then pounces and quickly kills it.

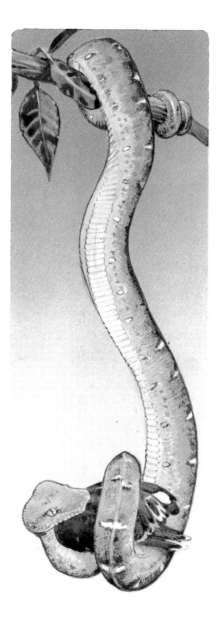

Pitcher plants trap insects which come to drink the sweet liquid round the plant's rim.

If an insect falls into the water in the plant and cannot climb out, the plant then eats it.

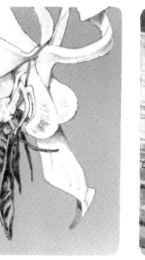

This flower spider hides inside a flower and catches moths as they look for pollen.

The bird-eating spider hides on the ground. It can kill a small bird with one bite.

The colour of the emerald tree boa acts as camouflage when it lies in wait for birds.

The Death of the Jungles

All round the world jungles are being cut down and destroyed.

Every minute, another 50 acres of trees are felled and cleared.

Many jungle tribes make clearings in the forest. They chop down trees and burn them.

Then they grow crops. But the soil is soon worn out and they have to make a new clearing.

Other people make a lot of money by chopping down the trees so they can sell the wood.

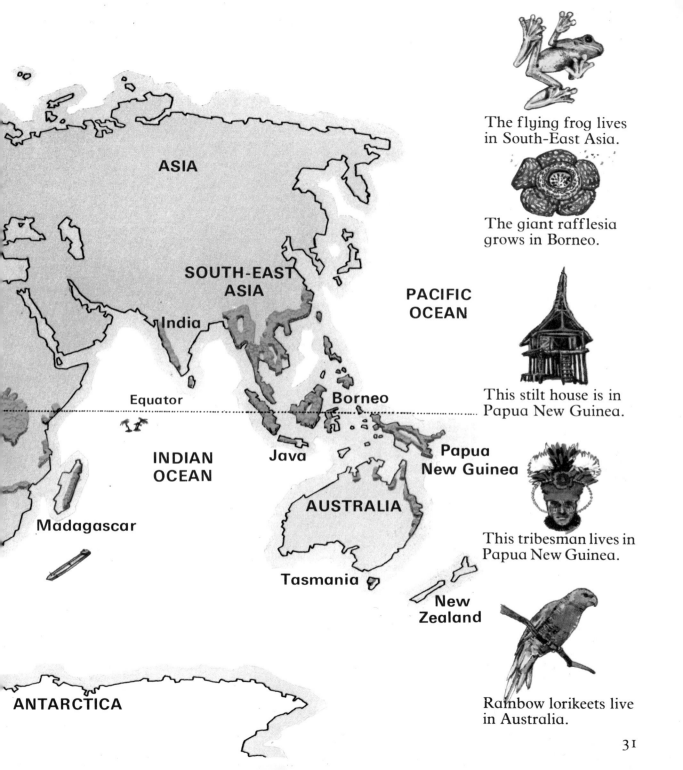

ASIA

SOUTH-EAST
ASIA

India

PACIFIC
OCEAN

Equator

Borneo

INDIAN
OCEAN

Java

Papua
New Guinea

Madagascar

AUSTRALIA

Tasmania

New
Zealand

ANTARCTICA

The flying frog lives
in South-East Asia.

The giant rafflesia
grows in Borneo.

This stilt house is in
Papua New Guinea.

This tribesman lives in
Papua New Guinea.

Rainbow lorikeets live
in Australia.

31

The Big and the Small

In the jungle some animals and plants are much bigger than usual. Others are very, very small.

The African Goliath frog is almost as big as the tiny Royal Antelope.

A Cuban Bee Hummingbird is only just bigger than a bumble bee.

The giant anaconda and this small tree snake both live in the jungle.

The cassowary from New Guinea is too big to fly.

Some jungle trees may grow as tall as 60 metres.

© Usborne Publishing Ltd 1980
First published in 1980 by
Usborne Publishing Ltd
20 Garrick Street
London WC2 9BJ, England

Published in the U.S.A.
by Hayes Books,
4235 South Memorial Drive,
Tulsa, Oklahoma, U.S.A.

Published in Canada by
Hayes Publishing Ltd
Burlington, Ontario

Published in Australia by
Rigby Publishing Ltd
Adelaide, Sydney, Melbourne,
Brisbane, Perth

Printed in Great Britain by
Waterlow (Dunstable) Ltd.